THE TORTURE

By
BOBBY BROUILLARD

Table of Contents

Introduction

Once, Tower of Fangs and Death Rose were fighting over turfs, because of Mark and his wife Brit. They wanted to control the werewolves. So, when Brit died, he had no one to love. So, he went to the elders of the Death Rose and made a treaty with them and they said, "Yes we will have a treaty with you. Our halfway mark is by the river, do not cross it unless you have permission by us." Mark, Brit and Wendy started the Tower of Fangs. They were full-blooded vampires and one day Wendy went on the Death Rose turf but had permission from a werewolf named Steven Scar. They were seeing each other.

One day Mark was walking and saw Wendy coming back on the Tower of Fangs turf and Mark said, "What are you doing?"

Wendy said, "I am pregnant with a boy. Me and Steven Scar named it Ponyboy."

One night Mark had a friend named Marie, he called her and asked her if she could kill Steven Scar. That night Wendy went into labour and gave birth to a boy named Ponyboy, with one eye blue and the other one yellowish.

While that was going on, Marie was walking and saw a girl and a guy. She walked over and asked him what is your name he said, "My name is Steven Scar." Then Marie punched him as hard as she could, breaking his nose and tossed the girl out of her way. Then she grabbed Steven's head and snapped his neck. Then she ran away where you could not find her.

Back with Wendy and Mark, the baby went into Mark's hands, went into another lady's hand and Mark shut the door and locked it. Then he said to Wendy, "Rest in peace," and took a knife to her heart.

Seventeen years later, Ponyboy was all grown up, living in a town with brothers, a sister, his adoptive mother and his father.

1

TORTURE

Chapter 1

Once on a nice summer day, a boy named Ponyboy was outside just having his daily walk around the block, just thinking his day through wondering what I wanted to do today. Then his cell phone rang. He answered the phone and said, "Hello who is this."

The girl on the phone said, "It is me pony boy, Cherry your friend."

"Oh, hi Cherry, how are you?"

Cherry said, "Ponyboy, I am doing fine."

"What are you going to do today, Cherry."

Cherry said, "Well I was planning to go to see my friends at the mall." While Ponyboy was talking to Cherry, a person named Marie came out of the shadows. Ponyboy was shocked and his cell phone dropped to the ground. You could hear Cherry saying "Hello Ponyboy are you there".

While that was going on, Ponyboy said, "Why did you startle me while I was talking to someone on the phone."

Marie said, "I am sorry. My bad for scaring you. I was just running away from someone attacking me."

Ponyboy picked up his phone still having his eye on Marie, looking at her, realising that something was wrong with her. While he picked his phone up, he asked her, "Why are you covering your neck?" Marie said, "Because I have a neck problem."

Meanwhile, Cherry is on the phone saying, "Helloooooooo is anyone there."

Ponyboy said, "I need to let you go for right now. Someone is hurt; I need to bring them to the hospital. I love you."

Cherry said, "I love you too."

Ponyboy hung up the phone. While Ponyboy and Marie were going to the hospital, back at Cherry's house, she was very upset with Ponyboy for hanging up on her. She felt hurt and alone. Her house phone rang. "Hello Cherry, it is your friends." About this time, it is nine o'clock in the morning.

Cherry said, "I will be there in a minute, at the mall." Cherry hung up the phone and went to take a shower. In those minutes, a person was taking out a tool to break into her house. He got in and stood in the shadows waiting for her to come out of the shower. The shower shut off. She was out of the shower with her towel wrapped around her body. She opened the bathroom door and saw some spotted blood on her floor. She carefully took her blow dryer and picked it up into her hands for a weapon; walking carefully out of the bathroom door, into the hallway of the house looking around where the blood was coming from. She followed the blood trail and came up empty in a corner where it was dark. She turned around, walking away.

A dark figure climbed down the wall and grabbed her. He said, "You are my woman to be, so that you can see my torture, what I went through." He took his sharp teeth and bit right into her.

She was trying to fight and she swung her blow dryer at his head and missed because she was in too much pain. Then she dropped to the floor screaming, holding her neck while she was bleeding and seeing images of the person that bit her, and of his past, and how he became a vampire.

While she was on the floor, the vampire named Mark Cola screamed over her and said, "Finally it is finished. She is born again." Then he hides in the shadows waiting for her to rise.

Meanwhile, back with Ponyboy and Marie, Ponyboy said to Marie, "Do you need to go to the hospital?"

She said, "Yes I might?"

Ponyboy said, "I will take you to the hospital then. So, the doctor can see whatever is wrong with your neck problem."

She said, "There is nothing wrong with my neck. It just hurts because there are two holes in my neck and they are both bleeding."

Ponyboy picked up Marie, walked her to his car and put her in the front seat of the car. He closed the door of the car and then opened his side to get in. He started the motor of the car and drove off to the hospital.

Meanwhile, about half an hour down the road, the dark figure was hiding in the shadows watching Ponyboy and Marie driving away. Marie looked over and saw the figure; she said to Ponyboy, "It was not the one that attacked me. It was probably a person walking in the woods, walking around."

So, after about a two-hour drive to the hospital, Marie went into a shock and Ponyboy told her not to worry. We are there. I will get you some help. He opened the car door and saw a doctor in the hospital parking lot. He said, "I need you to help me because this lady, Marie, is in shock." He said, "She has some kind of two holes in her neck."

So, the doctor rushed her to the hospital. Ponyboy was running with them, right behind them going into a room. The doctor put some needles in her arms. The doctor came out and said to Ponyboy she was fine. She just needs some rest. I put some blood into her body so in a couple of hours or more, she will be fine.

Ponyboy said, "What about the two holes in her neck."

The doctor said, "They are just little marks that will heal up."

So, around nighttime, about eight o'clock, Ponyboy heard a noise in Marie's room. The door was locked so he slammed his shoulder against it and the door broke open. Then when he was done trying to get up from breaking the door down, he stood up and saw Marie in the window staring at him with her sharp teeth that looked like vampire's teeth.

Marie said, "Well I am free from the human side now. I can live free and forever". Marie then leapt out the window onto the ground without a scratch on her. She looked up at Ponyboy and winked at him, then ran off into the night, while Ponyboy looked at her out of the window.

Then Ponyboy called Cherry on his cell phone. No one answered the phone at all. He then ran out of the hospital to get into his car and drove away. Then as he was going down the road when he turned the corner, he slammed on the brakes hard and got out of the car to see whom he hit. He hit a wolf. Ponyboy said "Damn, what is going on tonight with me. Cherry is not answering the phone. I saved a vampire. What else is next"? Therefore, Ponyboy then took the wolf, picked it up and put it on the side of the road. Then he was in the car and turned his head. When he saw no one thereafter, Ponyboy said, "What a weird night it's been". Then he got into his car to drive to Cherry's house in a rush.

Chapter 2

While Ponyboy is driving to Cherry's house in a rush Cherry's house with Mark and Cherry, Mark says to Cherry, "Raise my wife, that the humans killed, rise from the dead." So, Mark saw Cherry rise from the floor onto her feet. With her yellow eyes and her sharp teeth, she is now his wife until she dies. So, one of the scout vampires, Mike Lomer, came back to Mark and said "I... I... I saw the girl that you bit while you tried to finish the ritual over her, and she kicked you in the nuts."

Mark said, "Who else was with her?"

Mike said, "It was a man."

Mark said, "Hmm, okay then let's go out and feed with my wife Cherry, she has not fed on any blood yet." Therefore, Mark and Cherry went into the night, walking out the door. Mark said to the scout vampire Mike, "Find Marie and bring her to me and the man that was with her." The scout vampire Mike went into the night to find Marie and the man.

While everything was going on, Ponyboy pulled up to Cherry's house and saw the door broken off the frame. Therefore, he yelled Cherry's name and she did not answer at all. He went into her house to see if she was sleeping or doing other things. When he got to the top of the stairs, he saw blood on the floor and followed it. When he got to the end of the blood spots he was in rage of the blood that was there. Again, he yelled out her name, "CHERRY where are you," repeating over and over, yelling her name. Therefore, he left and drove off to go back to his house.

White Marie was in the woods to hunt for food, she saw two people walking in the night. She looked at them very carefully and moved quietly in the woods to attack them. She leapt in front of them and ripped one of their throats apart.

Then the other person said, "You would not like the taste of me"

Marie said, "I might like it." As the blood around her lips and chin dribbled down her neck, she then attacked the human. Kicked him in the chest and dodged out of the way when he tried to hit her in the face. Then she ran away from the attack and kept on running in the woods.

Meanwhile, the wolf that was going to the hospital and was hit by a car then put on the side of the road; got up and left. She went into the woods; as soon as she tried to walk on her left foot, she knew that she had broken her foot. Therefore, she limped her way to the cave where her clan was living. She had a long way to go but she saw a cave to rest in. She walked up to the entrance and smelled the area to see if it was safe to sleep in. She then walked in because she knew it was safe in there. Therefore, she can sleep in a safe area.

While Amanda Rose was sleeping in the cave, safe, Marie was trying to find a place to clean up. So, she was walking around and her eyes caught a place; it was a school that was closed and dark. Therefore, she broke the chains. off the door to get in. She looked around the area she was at. No one was in the area so she went into the school and looked for a place to clean herself up. By the time she was looking around her eyes were tired, but she managed to keep herself awake, to find the shower. She went around the corner. She then took off her bloody shirt and pants, and threw them in the corner of the shower while she was walking into the warm steamy water; she saw a shadowy person watching her. She finishes what she is doing but is aware of the person being there. She let the warm water hit her body and her hair; the blood that was dripping off her body and her face onto the floor draining down the drain. Then she pulled her hair back while it was wet, nice and tight. Then she put on her shirt and pants and she said, Well forget the shirt I will just wear my bra. In addition, my pants with my shoes." She turned around very quickly and saw a person Coming her way; she stood there and waited for them to come closer to her.

It was a police officer, who said to her. "What are you doing here?"

7

Marie said, "Oh I was just taking a nice long walk around the block with my naughty self; do you want to play with me?" While she was talking, the police officer was getting hot and bothered. So, Marie walked up to him very slowly.

He said, "Stay back or I will shoot." She kept on coming and she got to him. Started to undress him with her hands.

He said to her, "You have very cold hands."

She said, "I know I have a very cold heart too." After that, she then said in a whisper, "Watch your back, it might bite you where you do not want to be bitten." She then kissed him on the neck and said, "You need to leave because I am not a lady you want to be messing around with, or even touching you. Please leave."

James said, to Marie "I will leave you alone.

However, why do you not want me to touch you

or mess around with you?"

Marie said, "Just leave, please".

So, James left the school area where she was and James looked back to see if no one went inside of the entrance that he came out of.

So, she looked for a place where she was to sleep because it was almost daylight. The sun was peeking up in the window. So, she went to look around to find another place to stay. However, in her head, she was thinking why did I let that person go, that was my food to eat and drink. Why did I let him go? That was going on in her mind, just thinking that. So, she found a place in the school kitchen to be safe. She looked at her body and saw a mark on her right arm; it had a tower with two fangs on top of it. Nevertheless, talking to herself, saying I never had this mark before so why now. Therefore, after deriving a conclusion, she was nodding off to sleep.

Back in the cave where Amanda was sleeping being safe so that she could heal most of the broken foot. "It feels like it is still broken," she said to herself. So, she tried to walk on it and managed to limp on the left foot a little bit.

She walked outside the cave to find some sticks to straighten out her foot from not moving. She managed to put it together and put it on her foot. As soon as she put it on, she knew how long they had to go to get to her clan cave where they stayed. She said to herself aloud, "Puck this I will find a place to fix myself and make friends to join my clan and to branch off of us." Then she left the cave. She said to herself "It is four more days before the full moon starts up and I need to find this lady that snapped my friend, Steve Scar's, neck." She remembers looking at her and saying, "WOW she is very strong for herself." So, she had to climb through the woods to see if she was around.

So, about a half-hour into the woods and smelling around, there was no sight of her in the woods. So, she was out of the woods, onto the sidewalk limping her way around trying to find the lady; smelling her and looking around. So, she kept on looking and then came up to a gas station, limping her way over there. Finally. about two minutes later, she was near the gas station, went inside and said, "I need to use your bathroom to fix my wound on my foot."

So, the clerk looked down at her foot and saw it was bleeding a lot and he said, "You need to go to the hospital for that, it looks bad."

She said, "I do not care about the hospital" in a mean voice, "I care about me taking care of me, not the hospital." Her eyes started to glow yellow because she was getting pissed off at the clerk. So, she grabbed the clerk and said, "I am going to use your bathroom." With her eyes Blowing yellow and her teeth showing, she put one of her hands up in the air with her claws out and said, "You are to watch over my cave and my clan to teach them." She then scratched him with her claws to change him. Then she bit him on the neck to mark the property of hers.

So, while the clerk was going through pain, she went to the bathroom to find something and came up empty and checked the other one, when someone answered, "Yes, excuse me. I am in here," the person said.

So, Amanda said to the person "I need to use this bathroom because the other one is not working well."

The person that is inside the bathroom said, "I will be out in a few minutes."

So, Amanda got more aggravated with the person in the bathroom so she put all her aggravation into her fist and put it through the door. She looked through the hole and said to the girl "Now I can see you, lady. Come out or I will break down this door," Amanda then said to Herself, "I am going to keep myself from not breaking down this deer."

So the lady said, "I am not coming out of your crazy hitch, you psycho." So, then Amanda flips her lid, puts her weight into the door, and breaks it down. She went after the lady. She was in the corner of Amanda and said, "Are you playing with my judgment and questioning me when I said, "I can see you lady, come out or I will break down this door. Do not question that miss, please. She gave the lady a kiss on the cheek. Amanda then lifts her head from her cheek and raises her hand in the air with her claws showing, slashing the lady's face up, blood splashing all over the wall. Then Amanda left the gas station with the clerk that hit and slashed across the chest and the lady that she slashed across the face, she looked around and found a car that was the lady's that was still running. All Amanda said, "I have to put these two in the car so that they can wake up safe in the cave and tell them what they need to know." Then Amanda forgot that she was looking for Marie to talk to her and see how she was doing. To ask Marie why she was killed. my friend, Steve, who was joining my clan of Death Rose.

So, Amanda drove off to the cave. While Amanda was driving to the cave with two people in the car, about 3 hours away from where Amanda was, and James and Maria were at a school.

James was outside of the school sleeping in his car when all of a sudden, a human jumped onto his police car screaming with his face all Bashed up with scratches on his face. James said to the person, "Who attacked you, was it an animal or a wild dog?"

The person said with a silent whisper and with the last breath he took, "It was an animal but it looked like a wolf."

James then heard someone coming out of the woods. So, James pulled his gun out, a young boy came out of the woods, and James said, "What is your name sir?"

The young boy said, "My name is Matthew am looking for someone named Amanda Rose. You ever heard of that name before."

James said, "No never heard of that name at all; there Matthew." Then James said, "I heard of Marie, a lady who is living in the school right now."

By this time, when Marie is sleeping in the school people are going in and out of the school.

So, Matthew looked at James and spoke. "Hmmm okay, I will go and look to see if you are fighting. If you are right, you can keep your life. If you are not right; I will take your life." White Matthew was saying that his eyes were glowing red.

James said, "Okay, but why are your eyes Blowing red? What are you?"

Matthew said, "You will not understand what I am." Matthew walked across the street to the school; seeing the people that were going into the school.

However, inside the school Marie was sleeping in the high refrigerator, keeping herself nice and cooled off. So, Marie heard a noise outside of the refrigerator, of a girl's voice and a man's voice talking about someone breaking into the school last night.

James said, "It was just a thug that was just being himself. So, I arrest him."

She knew it was James that was there. Then she listened more and heard another man's voice, but never heard his voice before. She smelled the area to see if James was in trouble and she smelled a werewolf nearby. It wasn't a friendly werewolf that she knew; it was looking for someone. So, she waited to see if someone had her feet while James was trying to catch up to her. Marie looked in a window to see if there was any shadow outside; so that she could flee from the school where she murdered a werewolf. Marie saw a shadow by James's car but more leading that way to his car and in the woods. Marie then kicked the door open and leapt into the shadow, jumping from one to another. She made it there, but when she made it there, she stopped and smelled. She said to herself, "There are new breeds around. I need to find Amanda quick to talk to her."

Chapter 3

Mark and Cherry were walking around through town holding hands Mark said to her "Love you Cherry you are my wife that I love and forever."

Cherry said, "I love you too Mark". So, they kept on walking when they saw a group of people talking coming out of the bar and walking their way.

Mark said to Cherry, "Here are some people that we can feed on for the night"

Cherry said, "Let's eat then. Let's not wait my love." So, the people nodded to Mark and Cherry. The man and the lady just gave them a nod of their head. Mark and Cherry went around the corner into the alley to make it where they left. So, Mark peeked out to see where the people went, they were going into an apartment building. So Mark said to Cherry "This is our chance to feed for the night before the sun rises up."

Cherry said, "Okay let's get them and feed off of them. I am getting very hungry waiting."

So, she went running out when Mark said "Hold on wait for me." Cherry did not answer, she kept on running towards them with her blue eyes glowing and her fangs out nice and share waiting to bite the people that she was attacking. Mark is running behind her trying to get her attention in her head not to go after them by herself "Wait for me."

Cherry heard the voice in her head but did not answer it. She kept on running. Cherry finally got there where all the people whore at. One Person said to Cherry "Ha who are you? What are you doing in there?"

13

Cherry said, "I am here to talk to you and to drink all your people's blood and splash it all over the walls." She then showed herself to them when she came out of the dark shadows leaping towards them with her sharp fangs gushing for their blood.

Cherry grabbed one of them and put her fangs into his throat ripping his throat apart then one lady said "You're a vampire you're evil to us kill her you guys."

Then Mark came leaping out and grabbed the lady that said kill her. He bit her on her face and he dragged his fangs across her face.

Then Cherry started to claw all the other people up gashing them with her claws and biting them, blood splashing everywhere. So, she had fun killing everyone but not the lady. She went over to her where Mark had his fangs in her neck. Cherry said to her, "You are going to be my daughter to teach my vampires that I will breed. To learn them to hunt their food well."

The lady said, "No I will not do that. You will have to torture me first before I will do anything like that."

So, Cherry then told Mark to Change her and I would do something to her when we went back to our house. So Cherry, Mark and the lady that is knocked out from lack of blood are walking to their house and the sun is almost coming up so Cherry and Mark are quickly running to the house to get there safe. So, they made it barely when the sun came up burning Cherry's finger and she said, "Hawwwwwwwwwww, Mark we need to be on time next time so that I will not burn my nice hands or fingers."

Mark said, " Fine we will be home on time. my love, we will." So, they went to put the lady downstairs and woke her up in a cell that was dark. They whipped her and cut her back up with a razor whip and a regular whip then took her, chained her to the wall, and left her there. So, they left the cell and slammed the door where it was dark.

The lady was lifting her head to see what was going on. She smelled something coming her way. It was a human very old. She said, "Are you one of me,"

He said, "No I am just a human."

The lady said, "Do you know how to escape from here in this cell."

The old man said, "Yes but it is going to cost you."

She said, "What is it going to cost me?"

The old man said, "Just a little something Some things that will you do for me."

The lady said, "Well okay, just for me to get out of here. Okay, do not be long."

So, the old man said, "We will do it in a little bit because they will be coming soon."

So, Mark and Cherry came down the stairs to see how the lady was doing. They said to her. "How are you?"

The lady said to Mark and Cherry, "Well I am healing very slowly but doing fine. So how are you doing Mark and Cherry?"

They said, "We will be going to hunt for our food while you are staying here and eating rats for your dinner."

The lady then spit on Cherry and said to her "If I get out of here alive, I will bill you right down the middle of my vampire life."

Cherry said to the lady "You will never get out of here. You will grow old like the old man that is in the comer. You will grow old like him and die here." So, Cherry and Mark said to the lady and the old man "We will be back from feeding and we might come back with something for you." They shut the door very quietly and went upstairs talking to each other.

15

So the lady said to the old man "We need to get this done tonight."

The old man said, "Okay let's do it then."

So, the lady lay down on the ground looking at the old man getting undressed and kissing her on the stomach all the way up to her lips. He then unbuttoned the lady's shirt to see her nice chest area. Then unzipped her pants to see her thong that was already nice and wet. Then the old man unzips his pants, sticks it in her, and starts to pump away. Then after a while, he got finished with what he was doing he said, "Go through that wall that has a crack. You will see it, and push it open. You will then be outside of the woods. Then just find a place to clean up."

So, the lady said, "Thank you for everything." Then left him there, while this was Doing on back with Ponybay going back to his house he was driving to his house mad at himself wondering. Why he did not be there for her instead of being at the hospital with Marie the vampire? Then he thought to himself, but I did a good thing. Then he got more mad, then looked in the mirror and saw on his arm the tower and the two fangs and one on the other arm he saw the black rose. He stopped the car about 5 minutes from his house to say to himself who would do this to me?

Then he thought to himself and remembered that his mom told him that she was a vampire and that she was seeing a man who was a werewolf. So, they said you are part vampire and werewolf. It is a wonderful gift. When he remembered that, he went back into his car, and drove to his house.

Ponyboy got to his house took off his shirt, socks, and pants and went into the shower to relieve the stress that he had all day and night while he was in the shower.

Mike saw the door open and saw the car that Ponyboy was driving, the one he saw him in. Mike then walked into the house and the door was open he looked around and heard that someone was in the house he said to himself, "Might be him in that room right there." He

Pointed at the room he was talking about Walking towards the voice. So, he waited outside of the door for him when he opened the door.

Ponyboy shuts the water off and wraps the towel around his waist covering his private area, he then opens the door and sees a man standing there looking at him. Ponyboy said, "Who are you? And what are you doing in my house?"

Mike said, "I am here to bring you to my master so he can talk to you and bring you life." Mike looked at Ponyboy, smelled the area, and found out that he smelled like a wet dog and vampire smell and gave a dirty look to Ponyboy.

Ponyboy said, "What is the matter? Why you do not like what you smell in the air? Are you very scared that it might bite you in the long run?"

Mike did not say anything he just looked at Ponyboy.

Ponyboy then said, "What do you need? You worthless vampire, before I rip you into pieces."

Mike then quickly said something "I am here to break you in half and kill you forever."

Ponykey said, "We will see about that." Ponyboy laughed and started to go into pain, changing into a half-breed of vampire and werewolf standing up.

Mike looked at Ponyboy

Ponyboy said, "Are you in fear of me now? You weak full-blooded vampires. You cannot beat me. I was born this way and I love the way I am." He then took his claws and ripped Mike's face open with three swipes of his claws then he said to Mike "Do me one thing. Tell your master I will see him soon and I am going to kill him for what he did to my friend Cherry," Ponyboy then took both of his hands and his claws and marked his neck to know that he had given him a chance. Ponyboy said, "Get out of my house before I rip you apart and make you my dinner."

Mike then left Ponyboy's house in a flash. running into the night, back to his master's house.

Ponyboy rested for a while, getting back to himself and looked in the mirror saying damn I need a shower again. So, he went back in the shower to clean up.

Then he came out and went upstairs to call one of his friends. The phone kept on ringing and ringing and finally, Ponyboy hung up the phone, went down the stairs, and said to himself should go for a nightly walk to catch up on stopping in to see my friend or bumping into them. Bo, Ponyboy walks out the door, closing the door behind him, and goes for his nightly walk, looking around to see if that little snake, Mike, is watching him. There was no one around but the people walking at night.

Ponyboy was walking when he saw two ladies walking towards the park with a question mark on the back of their shirts. He said to himself, why are these two girls wearing a question mark on the back of their shirts? So, he sniffs the air and they are vampires of a new clan. He said to himself quietly, what new-age vampires are coming around my area? So, he went up to them and said, "Are you ladies new in this area?"

One of the ladies's said, "No I live about four blocks from here in a nice green house."

The other lady said, "I live with her too, she is my sister. So what about you sir where do you live?"

Ponyboy said, "Well it is too hard for me to explain to you two ladies. You might bite me and leave me for dead or for food." Ponyboy then showed his yellowish and blue glowing eyes at them.

The lady's looked at him and they showed their greenish eyes and sharp teeth. They know he was a vampire. They smelled him when he was walking right behind them. So, the two ladies leapt at him when he changed into his half-breed self, he ran towards them and grabbed one of them. The other lady bit him on the shoulder where blood was squirting all over him and her. She then picks up her head and screams out "This blood is very powerful."

He said, to the two ladies, "You like that blood, how powerful it is. Well, that is your last drink of it." Ponyboy then took one of the ladies and snapped her head and then took the other one and put his sharp nails right through her heart and ripped it out of her chest with blood Splashing all over him,

He then walked back to his place and said, "I am crashing for the night. Before I do that. I might take a shower and heal up." He went to open the bathroom door when he heard a knock on the door. He walked to the door very carefully without making noises. He got to the door and asked, "Who is this."

She said, "It is Crystal, I need some help. Please, I am all a mess can you help me."

Ponyboy smelled the area and knew it was a Vampire, but what kind of vampire? He opened the door and saw on her arm it was a tower with fangs the one that he had on his arm he quickly saw her all scratched up, and her shirt and pants were all ripped.

He asked, "Who did this to you?" She said, "I do not know. They were vampires, two of them. One was a girl with red hair and the other one with black hair. Please help me. I was locked up with an old man."

Ponyboy said, "I will help you. But you need to stay right here and I will be right back." Ponyboy knew she was a slave of this clan because she would not give up her friends, so she sacrificed herself for her friends, and that's why she became a slave vampire.

Ponyboy said to her "I am going to wash you up in the tub that I have in the bathroom." So, he picked her up, put her into the cold water, washed her up, and saw the deep cuts on her. He knows that she would be in trouble if he left her alone by herself. So, he said to her, "You can sleep with me for the night and we will try to find you a place to stay." Ponyboy asked Crystal do you want to stay here with me.

Crystal said, "Well I like you as a friend, you are very cute. Ponyboy had black hair built nice and thin about 5/9, 165 lbs." Crystal looked at him when he took off his shirt. She said, "Nice body,"

Ponyboy said, "Thanks, Crystal. You have yourself a good night."

So, in the meanwhile, Mike went back to the house, and knocked on the door; no one answered. He said, to himself "Well seems like they went hunting for their food or torturing more people downstairs." Mike heard something behind him. It was a lady with blonde hair, green eyes, and well thin. She said, "Who does this house belong to?"

Mike said, "I do not know I am just meeting someone here."

So, the lady said, "Where are you from?" Mike said, "I live around this bloody place but not in this house."

The lady said, "Well I think that you are lying to me. I smell it all over you."

Then Mike looked at her and saw the question mark right next to her left eye, a small question mark. He said, to her "You are a dirty little blonde lich that I could not smell your sense of a vampire."

She said, "No you couldn't because I had so much perfume on, that's why you could only smell the perfume that was on me."

Mike said, "You are a different vampire than us, you have green eyes."

She said, "Yes I am different. I am the new age of you. When I kill you with my hands."

So, Mike and the lady started to fight. Mike grabbed her and threw her up in the sky, he then flew up in the sky took his claws and scratched her face up. Then she slammed down into a house, trying to get up from it, but getting up slowly.

Mike was seeing it and he flew down there quickly. He got there and she was already standing up. She said, "It is my turn little scout vampire, the little down-ranking bitch." She spun around and took a knife out while she was spinning. She sliced Mike's throat then took the knife and stabbed him in the heart straight through, leaving him there in ashes. She said, "Another old-age vampire bites the dust." She then went on to the roof to see if anyone else was like him. She said to herself "I might just Jump down, pick up Mike's dust, and keep it need to use it for something."

So, she looked at the house that he was waiting at, and remembering the house and the street that she was in, she hoped so.

She then left with Mike's ashes and walked down the road when Mark and Cherry were coming back from their nightly walk with a little bit of blood on their shirts. Then the lady smelled the air and did not find anything on Mark or Cherry, just a little scent on them that they were something and she could not find out what.

Mark said to the lady "You are out here so late. It is very dangerous out here."

She said, "I can hold myself in a fight if someone attacks me, sir."

Cherry said to her "I hope you can be aware of your enemies that will sneak up on you."

The lady said, "I will keep an eye out for my enemies of the night." So, the ladies walk the other way than Mark and Cherry. Mark and Cherry walked down an alleyway to get home because they felt that someone was watching them very closely, So, Mark said to Cherry. "Would you want to split up and meet each other in the back of the house?"

Cherry said, "Okay, I will do that, split up and meet in the back of the house, that is fine with me."

So, they split up and the lady said, "Where are they going?" She then said, "Forget it I am not running them both down at all. I will go back to my questionable clan and get some rest for the next night."

Mark and Cherry made it back to the house without any problem. They went to the front of the house and saw a trail of ashes that belonged to a vampire. Mark smells the air and says to himself "It was a fight here, in the sky and ended up over there in someone's house." He then tried to see who it was. The clear thought that it came to be it was Mike and the lady. He said to Cherry "Remember the lady that we were talking to. she, the one that killed our scout vampire Mike."

Cherry said, "Oh well he was going to die soon. So we just have to kill her when we see her again that's all." So, Cherry and Mark went into their house and went downstairs to see the lady that they made into their slave, and did not see her. They said to the old man "Where is our vampire slave?"

The old man said, "I do do not not know. She took a rock and knocked it over my head and I passed."

So, Cherry and Mark said, "We need to go to bed and wait till tomorrow night to see where she is at. It is going to be sunlight right now. So, we need to go to bed and wait. She will not make it out there in the world without someone being there for her." So, they went to bed, cuddled with each other, and said, "See you in the nighttime."

Chapter 4

Marie went into the woods a little bit to catch her breath. She saw so many people looking for her she was getting very pissed off. However, in the corner of her eye, she saw a car driving very slowly through the school area. Marie smelled the air and found out the person in the Car was a werewolf. She then walked up to the car and said, "I need a ride lady bod." Marie looked at her and glowed her eyes at her and Amanda took her eyes and glowed her eyes at her.

Amanda said, "I am your friend that you ran into, in the woods, and you killed my friend, Steve, the one that I was going to put in my clan."

Marie said, "I am sorry that I did that, but we got other things to do and worry about. Our clan sticking together and getting together at once. Because out there is another clan of werewolves, named destroyers, with two axes on their left arm. I ran into one named Matthew. He was looking for you, to destroy you where you were not coming back."

Amanda said, "Well I cannot go back to my clan yet because I need to heal my foot, because I broke it. I need a couple of more days. So, when the full moon comes in two more days feet will heal."

Marie said, "How are you doing? In addition, why are you so far away from your clan? About ton hours. You are supposed to stay between our turf and yours."

Amanda said, "I was coming to see you. And I am doing fine. I just wanted to tell you to watch your back, too, the destroyers are out looking for new turf, So there are the Questionables, they are the new ages. That's why I came all this way."

Marie said, "Let's go for a drive, so we can talk privately about more of this."

Amanda said, "I got a cave about four hours from here in the woods."

So, they get in the car and as soon as they did, Marie said, "What the fuck is this; all this blood. And the lady and the guy lying dead."

Amanda said, "These are my guards for my cave that I am going to build with my own clan. So that I can go back with them, to tell my master that I trained a couple of people."

So when Amanda and Marie left, James came out of the school and asked "Where is Marie, you guys."

One guy said, "I do not know, last I saw her over by the woods."

James said, "Get a deg crew together and hunt her down."

So, while that is going on Amanda and Marie are going to the cave four hours ahead of them. Marie said, "I need a dark area from not burning Into ashes."

Amanda said, "Ge in the back seat and put the four blankets on you so when the sun comes up you are not burned." So, Marie went to the back of the car and put the blankets over her with the two other people.

Amanda was driving, trying not to fall asleep, when she saw a human on the road hitchhiking with his thumb out. So, Amanda stopped far away from him, and she lifted her nose and smelled the air. It smelled bad. It smelled like a wet dog like me. She said to herself, "I do not have anyone helping me so I am going to go right by him and look at his left arm." So, she drove right by him and saw the two axes on his left arm. Therefore, she drove a little faster to the cave to keep Marie safe. When they are there, she will wake Marie because it is dark in there.

So, while Amanda was driving, her eyes were getting tired. So, she was about three minutes from the cave, they parked the car off the road but woke up the two people, and Amanda said, "You need to carry my friend Marie for me Because she is part of our treaty that the vampires and werewolves have. We have to take out for each other's back and not backstab each other."

So, they picked her up and walked the three minutes. So, they get there and Amanda goes into the cave to see if it is okay to enter, Amanda says, "It is okay you can put her down in the dark so she can wake up."

Therefore, they put her down and Marie woke up and said to Amanda "This is where you are living right now."

Marie said. "It smells a little bit in here. Can you clean it up a little so it will not smell bad in here?"

Amanda said, "Okay we can clean it up a bit for you and me, plus the other ones we are training."

So Marie said, "It is one more day before the full moon comes. So we need to train these new werewolves of Death Rose so they will be ready for the full moon when it comes."

Amanda said, "Okay let's go and train them, but wait until tonight so that we can rest this morning, Shay Marle."

Marie said, "Okay fine"

So, Amanda, Marie and the new Death Rose People went to sleep right next to Amanda and Marie. While Amands, Marne, the man, and the lady were sleeping, James was searching for Marie in the woods with dogs and the Policeman to see where she went.

James said, "Let's go to the north and keep following this path, it might lead us to her and the one that she or he was with. We will then arrest her for running away, or talk to her about what that thing was that attacked her." They get about halfway to the path and see bones and heads missing from people's bodies. James said. "Hold on, we probably went the wrong way. Oh, here is a path right here, going northwest." They followed James' lead on the path. They got halfway to the path when they saw more bones and people's heads on the sticks while walking the path to catch Marie and the other one with her.

So, the officers said to James, "Do you still want to go ahead or backtrack?"

James said, "We are not backtracking because they can escape or brush their tracks away that's why I am not backtracking, we are going forward. Now let's go."

The police officers kept on watching with James, with him leading the way to northwest Meanwhile back with Marne and Amanda, they woke up the man and the lady to see the sun go down. Amanda said, "Tonight is the night I go back to see my clan up in the northwest, where my cave is. However, my clan calls it a castle It's surrounded by water where you must dive in the water to find the entrance of the castle."

Marie said, "Okay thanks for the information I'll need when I must come and get you."

Amanda looked at the moon and said, "We have about two hours before I change into a werewolf, and the two, so we need to give them the information we know." So, Amanda and Marie sit down with the lady and the man. Amanda said, "First of all, what are your guy's names?"

The lady said, "My name is Becky." The man said, "My name is Fred."

Becky and Fred said, "What are we doing here?"

Amanda said, "You are a part of my clan and family. You are going to see them in twelve hours, does that answer your question for you Becky."

So Amanda and Marie were getting ready to train Becky and Fred for their first time changing into a werewolf, to keep them alert for when they do change. They train them for about an hour and forty-five minutes. Amanda said, "We have fifteen minutes before the full moon appears away from the clouds."

Marie said, "Okay let them rest before they must change into the werewolf form."

So, Fred and Becky went and rested for fifteen minutes before they had to go to their new home up in the northwest. About fourteen minutes later, Becky and Fred were screaming in so much pain, and yelling, while they were having their bones getting bigger inside and, in their shoes, and their clothing was ripping off of them, while they were changing into a werewolf.

Then Amanda changed into a werewolf and her foot was healing up before she went over to Becky and Fred to lead them the way.

Marie wrote on the ground saying to Amanda "Meet us and my clan, Tower of Fangs, at the field in the north close to your castle, so when we get in trouble, we have safety to go to okay."

Amanda nods her head yes and heads Herthwest with Becky and Fred to get to her Clan, Then Mane is going to find her clan. Maria said to herself, "Probably I will hang out in the Bark so the people of my clan can see me because I have never seen the leader before." So, Mari got in Amanda's car, drove off with it, and headed to the park. While she was driving, she was thinking about the boy who helped her out of going to the hospital and getting blood in her So, she kept her eyes on the road when the vampire jumped onto her friend's car. She slammed the brakes on and got out of the car. Marie said, "What the fuck are you jumping on my friend's car? What are you a stupid bitch?"

The lady said, "Not yet, when I drink your blood dries."

27

Marie looked at her and saw a question mark on her left arm. Marie said to herself "Hammmmmmm, what is she doing on the old-age vampire turn? She must be planning something with her clan." Marie said, "So are you here to kill me too, or looking for werewolves because you aren't getting any at all."

The lady said, "Well let me say my name is Brit, and I am here to kill all vampires that are old ages. Because I already killed a vampire in this Vass with his ashes that I am going to raise from the dead again."

Marie got pissed off and let her finish what she was saying. Then Maris threw a knife at her and said, "Let's do this between you and me. That is it, old vampire to new vampire age. That's all if you win you get my ashes, if 1 win you be my slave or I kill you"

Brit nodded her head yes; it will be fine Marie

So, Marie went after her without talking slashing her face and body up and Brit was fighting right back with her nails, Marie saw Brit taking a silver knife out to stab her with it. She spun around, took her arms, wrapped them around her neck, and snapped her neck and she fell down to the ground. Then Marie leaned over her and said, "The old-age vampires are powerful; not the new-age vampires."

Marie walked over to the vase and picked it up. Then I wondered if she was doing a rising from the dead: Mike's ashes in the vase; she needed to write it on something. So, Marie was thinking like a vampire smelling the vase then caught a glimpse of blood on the vase it was words that were in blood in vampire language that Marie could say it said, "Raise my enemy. Let the blood of the new age vampire Bow through your veins and become one of us through blood and through soul, I raise you from your ashes, my follower," Marie was surprised about it. If she can reverse the words.

She would wait until she was caught up with Amanda, later. So, she went back into her car got a blade and drove it through Brit's heart and Brit turned to ashes. Then Marie was in her car driving off and

28

when she tried to find the park to rest and get off her feet, and to look for the boy that helped her out.

She got to the parking lot and parked her car, getting out of the car. Then she walks a little bit and sits down on the bench. When she was looking around, she saw a car at a house that she knew, the car belonged to the boy that brought her to the hospital.

She went over to the house and knocked on the door. Marie said, "Hello is anyone home."

Ponyboy heard someone at the door and ran down the stairs and Crystal said, "What about me Ponyboy? My tub and my back that you were going to fix up with all the cuts."

Ponyboy said, "Well she is my friend that I saved and she likes me. So, I just helped you out that's it, you are just a slave of us."

Crystal just got out of the thus, put on her clothes, and went downstairs with Ponyboy. She sat down on the couch with her hands crossed.

Ponyboy went to the door and said, "When is this?"

Marie said, "It is me. You are the one that brought me to the hospital and I jumped out of it."

Ponyboy opened the door to see if it was true and it was. He said, "Come on in and sit down with me. Oh, I forgot, meet Crystal too. someone turned her into a slave."

So, Marie sniffs Crystal to see who changed her, Marie stepped back, and Ponyboy said, "What is the matter what's wrong Marie?"

Then Marie snapped out of it and she said, "It was a girl with red hair and a guy with black hair." Then Marie said, "I know the one with the black hair because he was the one that attacked me that morning that I bumped into you Ponyboy. But I do not know about the redhead girl, sorry."

29

Crystal said, "She said her name was like Cherry or something like that."

So, Ponyboy was very pissed off, his eyes were turning yellowish and blue.

Marie looked at him and said, "You are different brend than us, what are you Ponyboy"

Ponyboy then relaxed and said, "My mom was a vampire and the man she was seeing was a werewolf. So, I am a different kind of breed than you ladies."

Marie said, "Well I got something for us to work on, at your house if you want, and Crystal can learn. It is a rising of our own vampire from the dead if you want." Ponyboy said, "Fine let's do it then, because after I am going to rip that guy's head off that changed her. He is mine; no one else."

Marie said, "You will get your chance to get your revenge for what he did to Cherry. Right now we need to do this ritual to get Mike back, to see where they are at." Ponyboy said, "Okay let's do this then, Marie. Crystal, can you watch the door for us please."

Crystal said, "Fine, I will watch the door for you Marie and Ponyboy. I will not let anyone in."

So, Marie and Ponyboy did a bloody circle and started the ritual of raising Mike back from the dead. Marie said, "Rise my clan brother let the blood of the old age vampire flow through your veins and become one of us, through blood and through soul, I raise you from your ashes my clan brother. So the lights were flicking in and out and the wind was blowing." Marie put Mike's ashes down on the floor, and they were coming together, forming Mike's body, and then the house went dark. Everyone was aware of what happened to the lights.

Mike said, "Thank you for raising me from the dead and keeping me alive.

Marie said, "Is that you, Mike?"

He said, "Yes, it is me, Marie, now you are going to be my master.

Mike then leapt in the air to grab Marie's throat. Marie moved out of the way and Ponyboy grabbed Mike's throat and said to him "If you ever try to do this in front of me, going after her. I will kill you myself. I brought you back to life, in my house, so you need to tell us where your leader is now. I need to talk to him, and ask him some questions, about these new-age vampires and the werewolves that are trying to take over our turf."

In the meanwhile, Amanda, Becky and Fred are heading towards the northwest to see their clan in the castle. Amanda was running through the woods with Becky and Fred when they saw some people who had two axes on their left arm. Amanda, Becky and Fred stopped and started to bark at them because they were on the Death Rose turf.

The three people, two males and one girl, turned into a werewolf and started to grow al Amanda, Becky and Fred. Amanda, Becky and Fred ran towards them very fast, leapt in the air with their mouths open and with their teeth showing ready to take a bite out of their throats. All three of them fended in front of the destroyers and started to attack them with their claws, and one of the destroyers took Fred's neck snapping his neck.

Amanda flipped out and leapt over Becky and the one that she was fighting, ran to the one that snapped Fred's neck. He was surprised by Amanda and she leached onto his mouth and ripped his whole nose, and his mouth out of his face. Amanda then walked away, looking at the other two that were coming her way. Amanda then growled at them and they ran away.

So, Amanda and Becky turned back into a human, but they had to put clothes back on. So, they did and walked all the way they had about seven more hours to go before they got there. It was getting morning and they were looking for a cave that was dark and safe, they were looking for a couple of minutes when they found one with water dripping from the wall or from the entrance. Amanda said, "It is safe for us to steep here. We have seven more hours before we get home. Let's go to bed okay."

So, they went to sleep safely but still were aware of the new werewolves and vampires out there.

Chapter 5

Mark and Cherry woke up from the Hap Cherry said, "What a bloody night. We have Bur slave on the run, mast holy eating everything in sight like we always do."

However, Mark said, "Someone most likely brought her in, one of us or someone out there is. So, we need to find the lady that we were talking to so that we can get Mike's ashes back and ask someone to raise him from the dead."

Cherry said, "Let's go and see the old man How stairs; where did my slave go off to? If she does not tell me, then we will find her the hard way, or go to a friend's house that I know."

Mark said, "You got a friend?"

Cherry said, "Yes I do Ponyboy"

Mark scratches his head in a confusing way trying to remember the name, Mark then has a very surprised look on his face and said, to Cherry, "That is a very old half-breed vampire mix, with werewolf; he is very old, Ponyboy, he is like 300 years old, but in human age, he is 31 years old. He is the only half-breed that is like that between the old-age vampires and werewolves. Cherry, he is very strong in straight."

Cherry said, "We need to see the bad man downstairs before we make our minds up about which one to find."

Cherry and Mark went downstairs and looked around for the old man, and did not see him at all out of the corner of the cell the old man said, "What are you looking for, me? 1 am right here in the dark corner. It is nice being in the dark."

Mark said, "Where did the girl go old man."

The old man said, "Like I said, she took a rock and knocked me out with it. That's all I know."

Cherry and Mark said, "Well we have to do it the hard way now. Go out there with other vampires and look for her, that's the plan."

The old man said, "Others are coming soon, to take over. I feel it in the air, new ages of us." Cherry and Mark said, "What did you say, old man?"

The old man said, "Nothing. You will see when you get out there."

So, Mark and Cherry said to the old man, "We will be back from our hunt for the lady that was in here with you." Mark and Cherry went upstairs and went outside to hunt for the lady. They took off, walking around the town to see where she Cherry asellus the and the Is shout 30 minutes Hom here the two near the park with paste that allows Mark to say, "Can you place their face-off Cherry?"

Cherry said, "Na. The only one to the tally that we have for our stave, that's it." However behind Cherry's head she knows that the lady is her slave, she was with vampires and with Ponyboy too, but she did not tell Mark at all. Because he did not know that Ponyboy was half-breed in the clan, so she kept it from him, Mark said to Cherry "Are you okay? Are you ready to get our slave back and have a nice meal?"

Cherry said, "Yeah I guess so let's go," But she knows this is a bad thing to do. She can feel It in her stomach, rolling around, that's how hard it is for her. However, she went with Mark to keep him company on the way there. So about 20 minutes into the walk, Mark saw someone in an alley looking at him. Mark said to Cherry "Stay here. I am going into this alley; someone is looking at me. I do not know who it is. So, it is very dangerous for you."

Cherry said, "What am I just your play toy, or am I your wife that you care about? If I am your wife, you should let me speak for my shit."

Mark was silent for about a minute, to see what he was going to say. Nevertheless, he did not say anything at all, just kept on looking at Cherry. He then went onto the alley very quietly, pecking around the corner, seeing a somewhat of a werewolf that smelled like a wet dog. Then his eyes caught a symbol of two axes crossing each other, Mark said to himself, "What are these new broods, or new ages of werewolves; because the ones we made a treaty with, have a black rose on their right arm?"

Mark quietly went back, got Cherry, and said to her, "There is a werewolf on our turf. Let's go and tear it apart together and feed off of it. So, they went back into the alley, walking very quietly. But Mark made a noise to let the werewolf snap his head around to look in that direction to smell who was there."

Mark said to Cherry in a silent whisper, "We need to leap and attack him if he comes this way."

So, Cherry said, "Okay. We will do that then. When he comes our way, which he is coming this way, Mark."

The werewolf was walking very slowly, to smell the good sense of a vampire. He turned the corner, and Cherry jumped on the werewolf's back, grabbed his head, and bit into his eye While Mack leapt in front of the werewolf, being attacked by Cherry. Mark then leapt up and sank his teeth into the werewolf.

The werewolf then, trying to grasp for air. found what little bit he had and howled for us to pack to come. Then Cherry said to Mark, "He just howled out, that means he called for his pack to help him out."

Mark let go of the werewolf and his teeth. He looked at Cherry and said, "Yeah I know that. They are not close they are about 20 minutes from here so that we can finish him off."

Cherry and Mark went up to the werewolf, took his head and snapped his neck. While they were doing that, two werewolves with marks of two axes crossing each other on their left arm were looking at them. One of them ran and leapt onto Mark, while he was eating.

Mark tried to throw him off him. It did not work, so Mark made another plan; he sunk his teeth into the werewolf's leg. The werewolf yelped and got off of Mark.

Mark got up and saw two werewolves on Cherry, chewing, and biting her with their teeth. Mark ran very quickly in front of Prom, last in the middle air, and came down with a fist to one of the werewolf's noses he yelled and let go of Cherry. Then behind Mark werewolf came running and took his whole body straight pummeled him to the ground and started to claw, bite and drag his body. Then after he knocked him out, the other one turned back into a human and put a sharp silver cross with a point at the end into Mark's heart. Mark Turned into ashes. The ashes burned as he turned to ashes.

So, about four of the destroyers of the werewolf pack left Cherry behind. One of them said, "She is dead. He is not coming back. Let's go and find the other old-age vampires, they will hopefully be more challenging than these two vampires."

While the four werewolves were, leaving Cherry was getting up very slowly. They were not going to turn around and see her getting up from the ground. She said to herself, "I need to find Ponyboy and the ones that are with him."

So, Cherry jumped up onto a building to see where the werewolves were going. They were Boing north to their castle. Cherry said to herself, "When I was a kid, I used to go to Castle up north. I hope that is not the area that they have their stan in."

Cherry continued to look for the lady and Ponyboy. She started to walk in the direction that she and Mark had been going, being very enraged and lost inside herself. So, she kept on watching. looking around; missing what she could have if she was a human. About 10 minutes later, she got to the park, looking around, seeing people having fun with each other and getting along with one another, laughing, smiling and joining one another's company. Then out of the corner of her eye, she saw a car that looked like Ponyboy's car, by a house. She went over to it very carefully. She went up the stairs and knocked on the door, but no one answered. So, she knocked again.

Chapter 6

Marie said, "There is someone at the door Buys."

Miko said, "I do not know about these new-age vampires or the werewolves; this is all new news to me. We need to get with our people and the werewolves, the Death Rose, so we can take these clans out."

Crystal said, "What about the door? Someone is at the door."

Ponyboy said, "They will go away after knocking after a while."

Mike said, "We need to get with the elders of the Tower of Fangs, so we can deal with the new-age clans. So, let's get together and do this."

Marie, Ponyboy, Crystal and Mike packed up and went to open the door and saw Cherry.

Ponyboy looked at her and said, "What are you doing here?"

Cherry said, "I am one of you, but the queen of you. Now, you are the master of use, because Mark died on the way here, to rip your head off Ponyboy."

Ponyboy said, "We are going to see the older of the vampires. So please get out of our way."

Cherry said, "Can I come in? Please, because it is very dangerous out there."

Crystal said, "That is her, the one that changed me into this hungry vampire thing." Crystal went up to her, grabbed her and spoke. "You need to control your anger before you change people. If I was a very or a backstabber, I would have ripped your throat to pieces when I left your house."

Marie said, "Are we all set to leave now, so our panties are not in a bunch with each other when we get together with the elders."

So, they went into Ponyboy's car, Marie, Mike, Crystal and Cherry. They started the engine up and started their way to the north to see the elders.

Meanwhile, Amanda and Becky got up from resting. Becky said, "It is nighttime. Let's go, Amanda so that I can see my new family."

Amanda said, "Can I get up and open my eyes before I make my decision if we are going or not."

Becky went out to get fresh air and Amanda came out there, with her knowing, she was in danger. Becky said, "I can take care of myself out here."

Amanita said, "Well do you know the symbols of use or our treaty symbols with the other clan we made a treaty with?"

Becky said, "Hammmm no."

Amanda said, "Okay then. You need to stay with me then. Now, let's go and see our family. So, they set off to the northwest to get together with their family, to have a big meeting then, after, with the elder vampires."

Amanda said to Becky "We got seven more hours before we get to our castle in the northwest. We will get there about 6 o'clock in the morning before the sun rises." While they were walking, about two hours in, they saw some trails of blood; fresh ones, Amanda put up her hand and said to Becky, "Stop right there. Someone is on our turf. I need to look around."

Amanda took off her clothes and her miscellaneous items. She got mad and started to change into a werewolf. Then Becky stepped in front of her, to guard her while she was changing. Then after that, Becky took off her clothes and her miscellaneous items; she hanged

39

into a werewolf and started to sniff around with Amanda. They ran for an hour and the blood trail ended. Right there, where Becky saw on her right, was some blood going into thick weeds. More, she took her nose and nudged Amanda, and took her head and waved it by the blood trail. So, they went towards the blood trail and sniffed their way about for twist hours, going to their castle, to go back to Death Rose clean...

There they saw about six destroyers with their symbols on their left arm, two axes crossing each other. Amanda and Becky looked at each other with a puzzled face. While Amanda and Becky were standing, they were trying to find a way around the six werewolves of the destroyer's clan.

James was about three hours away from them, with police officers too. James kept on searching for Marie and the other girl or him. So, they looked around and found some bones, fresh blood, and some clothes that Amanda and Becky took off to change into werewolves; the fresh blood trails thicker into the woods. James and the police officer followed the blood trail very carefully with their guns out in case they saw anything that they didn't know of. They went on for about one hour, following the trail and they lost it, hut and of the officers was looking around and saw some more blood trail. They went to and followed it all the way until it ended.

They got shouted at where Amanda and Becky were and James saw two wherewith looking at something. James said, "Do not move. I see about six more other ones, but they are different than them. They have different skin and fur on them." So, James and the officers waited for them to make their move.

Amanda and Becky were looking at them and Amanda and Becky's nose sense went off and they turned around and saw seven humans looking in their direction, but not at them.

James said, "The two werewolves are looking at us but they are looking away."

One of the officers said, "Let's go out there and attack them."

James said to the officer, "It is too dangerous. We will be meat for them. What I mean is we will be their dinner. So, do you want to go out there now?"

The officer said to James, "I do not care. I do not have a family to protect from these monsters or things." The officer ran out and opened fire at the werewolves, the ones that Amanda and Becky were looking at. The officer kept on firing at the werewolves. Then a bullet hit one of the werewolves from the destroyer's clone and his head turned around and saw where it came from and saw it came from a human.

The werewolf ran very quickly and jumped in the middle of the air when it was too late when he came down is attacked the human, Amends and Becky were there waiting for him. When he came down, they sin shed his face open and Becky ripped his throat open with her claws.

Then the other ones came when they heard a battle going on. They ran very quickly to the attack and started to attack whoever was there.

Then James and his officers came out and started to shoot with their guns. There was blood splashing and guts pouring and dropping from their bodies.

Amanda saw her clan coming, about seven of the Death Rose clan of the werewolves. Becky had two werewolves on her. She slashed one in the face and she came back around with her other claw and slashed him in the threat. Then the other one looked at her and ran.

Becky then, looked and let him go a little bit and ran very quickly and caught up to him. Then one of the Death Rose werewolves snatched him up and ripped his head off.

James was looking for the other wherewith, Amanda and Bucky; he only saw Amanda, but not Becky. He saw a lot more coming that fooled like Amanda and Becky's colour fur.

A were well that has a symbol of two axes crossing each other jumped on James. He did not know that he was coming. The werewolf stood over time, slashed his face open, and ripped his eyes out and blood was pouring very quickly.

Amanda turned her head and saw James dead on the ground. She ran over, jumped on him and snapped his neck. Amanda howled very loudly; everybody stopped in his or her tracks, and she turned back into a human.

Amanda said, "If you destroyers want to fight with us and the tower of fangs, meet us in three more days when the full moon rises rod over the moon."

Then all the destroyer's clan left and Amanda, Becky and the other ones helped everyone up that was on the ground. They got up to go to the castle. They walked for about two hours, jumped into the water, went underneath the castle and came up from the water.

Amanda and Becky looked around and saw a lot of werewolves walking around in the castle, some were human and some were in werewolf form.

So, Amanita walked to the elder's door and knocked on the door. The elder werewolf said, "Come on in. Make sure you shut the door."

Amanda shut the door and the elder said, "What is this I am seeing or hearing with the new-age werewolves. They want to fight us and try to take our turf over. Even the tower of fangs, too, our allies that we have a treaty with, and they have a problem with the question bins vampires of the new age. We had to tell the older of the Tower of Fangs that they had new-age vampires to watch out for. They will go on to your turf. They do not care if they die or not."

Amanda said, "We will get together with the elders of the tower of fangs."

The elder of the werewolf said to Amanda, "Let Marie, Ponyboy, Crystal, Mike and Cherry get to their house, so they can talk to their older vampire too. Then they will use our shortcut to come here to see us. Then we will make plans to fight them, new age clans."

While Amanda and Becky are talking to the elders of their clan, back in the north with Marie, Ponyboy, Crystal, Mike and Cherry are in the car heading to the house of their clan. About two hours away, they see five vampires of their ton fighting with the new-age vampires that have Question marks on their shirts, it was about eight of the questionable that were getting the best of the old-age vampires.

Marie stopped the car and got out of the car even Ponyboy, Crystal, Mike and Cherry too. All of them said, "Do you want to pick on vampires? Why don't you pick on us? You are on the Tower of Fange turf, not on yours. So, get off of our turf or be slayed by your enemy vampires, or by a werewolf that you do not like. So, you have two choices, new age vampires, make them now or die trying."

One of the new-age vampires; stepped up and said, "We will never take any offers from you little weak vampires; that cannot hold their own."

While the female vampire of the questionable was talking, Ponyboy was getting very upset and his eyes were turning yellowish. Marie looked back and saw him changing and she moved closer to him so that the new-age vampires could not see him changing.

Marie, Crystal, Mike and Cherry were in front of Ponyboy; he was in the back of them changing into a werewolf, Ponyboy said to Marte, "Get the way. I am ready to kill a new age vampire Again, MOVE NOW!" Ponyboy yelled out.

The female questionable looked at Marne when she moved aside and saw a ware wall behind her, Then the werewolf je at the female vampire, napped her arms off her body, and howled after, and the tower of fangs of the vampires stopped fighting, even the questionable vampires too.

Ponyboy turned hack into a human, held op the female head, and said, "Meet us in three days, when the full moon raises red over the moon. We will bring the Death Rose stan with us to fight the destroyers' clan. Be we will get hold of you when we get ready, until then, get off of our turf or I will start ripping heads off of your shoulders."

Ponyboy's eyes turned yellowish again and the seven questionable ran away and got off the Tower of Fangs turf quickly.

Marie, Crystal, Mike and Cherry said, "Are you okay Ponyboy?"

Ponyboy said, "It is very hard to control myself without having both sides going off. Because if it does, I cannot control it at all without someone knocking me out or killing me for good."

Crystal said, "But are you back to your regular self-Ponyboy?"

Ponyboy said, "Yes I am Crystal. Do not worry. You will know if I am not myself." So, the vampires come over to them, the same symbol on their right arm.

Ponyboy and Mike said, "It is okay. They are the family that are bringing us to see the elder."

Marie, Crystal and Cherry said, "Okay. We will go with you people because Ponyboy and Mike are going."

So, everyone started to walk towards the house but the vampires took a shortcut to the house, so people who passed them would know that they were walking and looking at the house.

Continuing the shortcut Ponyboy said, "Is this a new shortcut to the house? I do not remember this area."

Then she said, "Well, remember this corner, where your mother died giving birth to you, and It was your place to think when you grew up."

They turned the corner where they were talking about his mom's grave. And there it was there, the one with her picture. He started to get Pred off, and one of his eyes was turning blue the other eye was turning yellowish, and the Vampires were saying we've got to go to the house without Ponyboy. He will catch up with us later,

Crystal sold to Ponyboy, "Please come back to us when you San and control whatever is Inside of you."

Ponyboy said, "Crystal you need to leave. But I will keep that in mind. But you need to leave before I do something. Now go with our family to the house."

Crystal kisses Ponyboy goodbye on his cheek; walking away from him, leaving him there enraged at what happened to his mom.

Ponyboy then smashed his mom's tombstone ran into the thick woods, stopped in front of the river that has a waterfall looking straight down and he sat down.

Back with Marie, Mike, Crystal, Cherry and the vampires, they got into the house in the back way. The female vampire knocked on the door twice and a male person answered the door and looked out the little slot. He saw the female vampire, opened the door for her, and said, "Who are these people?"

Cherry spoke up and said, "I am your queen, not a vampire that takes Anders from little ants, hey you, doorman. Now, get out of my way. I will find my way to the elder's room with my vampire friends."

Cherry, Mike, Crystal and Marle were Walking into the house that looked very nice inside and Cherry said, "Do you know where the elders' room is? I need to speak with them. It is very important."

One of the vampires that were drinking blood, said, "Go up these stairs and take a right. Then, go down two doors. Then you will see the only double doors that are up there. Then knock four times."

Marie said, "Okay thank you, sir." Then Marie got everybody else that was with her and started going up the stairs.

When they got up the stairs one of the elders came out of one of the doors and said, "Follow me. I will bring you to our room. Oh, my queen Cherry! How are you doing?"

Cherry said, "I am doing fine. I just need to get these new-age vampires and werewolves off our back. Tomorrow tonight will be two nights before the full moon and the fight between the old ages and the new ages."

The elder and others were still walking when the elder said to Cherry, "Where is Ponyboy? Where is he?"

Cherry said, "It is a long story. He is not in his right mind of thinking, at all, for anyone to talk to him."

So, the other said, "Okay. I will see him if he comes back to us or we will see him at the fight."

So, they continued down the hall. The elder knocked on the double doors four times and an older female voice said, "Come on in. Watch your step when you come in."

The elder that was with Marie, Cherry, Mike and Crystal said, "Look straight head. It is a nice stick that is pointed for our enemy that comes through that door."

Marie, Cherry, Mike and Crystal went into the elder's room and saw a lot of vampires sitting there talking to the elder female vampire of the clan. Everyone was looking at Cherry, The Queen of the Old Age Vampires, and was looking at Mike. They were smelling how weak he was, and the elder vampire said, "He is ours, but he considers himself going on his own."

Then the mare elder said, "You need to keep him here with us, under our wing, or he will it killed."

The older vampire said, "Where is Ponyboy? He is supposed to be here with the four of you, not alone, you know it is two more days before the red full moon. It is going to be chases that night; blood against the new age and old age to see who is better than ever all."

Marie said, "We are here for something else: to tell you that we need to have a meeting with you and the Death Rose clan about the New Age Vampires and the werewolves. So, they will not get onto our turf. We set a date two days on the red full moon; we are fighting them if it is okay."

The female older said, "It is okay by me. 1 need to get a little bloody anyway. We will deal with the Death Ruse clan at the halfway mark of our turf agreement line." The female elder sat down, dipped her pen into the bloody ink and wrote on a piece of paper saying. To the elders of the Death Rose. We are going to meet with you at the halfway mark of our turf agreement line if you want us to cross that is fine. However, we need to talk business about these new-age vampires and werewolves sincerely the elder of the Flower of Fangs. So, when the older female was done with the lotter, she got up and snapped her fingers. A Mack crow came to her and she talked softly to the crow. The crow flew away into the night. The older said to Cherry the Queen of the Vampires, "We will need to be ready to go and meet with the Death Rose tomorrow night. So, get your rest for tomorrow okay."

Marie said, "Okay we will get our rest. But When Ponyboy comes our way, can you let me know and the others."

The elder female said, "Yes. We will let you know right away."

Meanwhile, Ponyboy standing there, looking at the waterfall straight down wondering if he should just jump but in his mind is saying to himself, "Do not jump. Your mom would want you to continue with your life as you are. And continuing the family blood of the half-breed in you." So, he did not jump. He just looked at the waterfall.

Then a very bad smell came across his nose, very quickly, to make him look around his turf and to make him move out of that area. He climbed up a tree to see who was on the Tower of Fang's turf. He stayed right there to see who was coming. A female vampire had a question mark on her lower left arm with three other vampires with her. So Ponyboy said to himself very quietly, "What should I do? It is four of them and one of me. But I am much stronger than they are. But I need to use my brain first, before my blood thrusts, I need to think quickly before they find our shortcut to our house."

The five vampires of the questionable were looking around, they did not see anything but the house and no entrance to the house. So, they turned around and left walking toward Ponyboy, So, Ponyboy got ready to attack them if they saw him.

So, they just went on by. But one of the vampires, the female, stopped and looked around and said, "There is something wrong. I do not feel right."

Then all of a sudden, the Tower of Fangs vampires jumped out and started to fight the five questionable vampires, slashing their faces, ripping their heads off, and blood squirting all around.

Then Ponyboy saw an elder vampire with Them on the questionable side. He was just talking to one of the vampires and he left. So, Ponyboy ran out, helped his clan out and started to fight with them and others. Ponyboy said to one of the vampires of his clan, "There is one going to sneak up on us. So, watch your back. I am going to fight with this older that is with them."

The male vampire of Tower of Fangs, said, "Just watch your hack Ponyboy. The one that ran, might just lead you into a trap. Just be careful, watch your step, that's all."

Ponyboy started to run up to the elder, but faked the elder of the questionable out and jumped over her and said, "What are you looking for ...me? You weakling vampires! You do not know what power is if it slaps you in the face. You are so overwhelmed with your blood that thrusting is pitiful just resolving on it. Just attack, like Tam going to."

Ponyboy then attacked the elder vampire of the Questionable; took the elder, picked her up and threw her into the thick woods. Then Ponyboy turned into a half-breed vampire werewolf and ran after the elder vampire she was attacking.

The elder vampire glided through the air and landed in the tree waiting for Ponyboy. Ponyboy was running through the woods when the elder vampire jumped on his shoulder and started to hit him in the head.

So, Ponyboy throws her off of him onto the ground. Then Ponyboy said, "You are mine now. I'm going to rip your heart out and feed it to the wild animals or you can serve the rest of your life in a cell without feeding off of blood."

The elder of the Questionable said, "I rather die by my enemy's hands than serve you halt-breed." Then the older spit on Ponyboy.

He got mad and looked at her with the blue and yellowish eyes. Then Ponyboy swung his arm fast, opened his hand quickly, ripped through the older skin, ripped out her heart and sold. "You are ashes now, be gone your weak elder vampire."

Ponyboy then ran back to see how the rest of his brothers and sisters were doing. One of his brothers came up to him and said, "It was throwing sisters and three brothers. One sister died and a brother too.

49

But Marie wants you back at the house because she is worried about you."

Ponyboy said, "I will be there in a minute. I am trying to find out who killed my mother. She did not die right here because this was her secret place, with her werewolf boyfriend who is the lead of the Death Rose clan."

Ponyboy's brother of the clan said, "We have one more night before we fight the questionable and the destroyers of the new ages. However, we are going to the northwest tonight to see the Death Rose can and talk to the elders there to make plans to destroy these two clans that are coming on our turf whenever they want to."

So Ponyboy and his brothers and sisters went back to the house and the older of the vampires said, "About time you came back Ponyboy. We've been worrying about you, even Marie and Crystal too. Oh, I forgot and the others that were with you."

Ponyboy said, "Where are they?"

The elder female stepped up and said, "They are safe. I will bring you to them."

So, Ponyboy walked up the stairs and followed the female elder to the door. The female elder knocked on the door and Marie said, "Who is this?"

The female elder said, "It is me and Ponyboy at the door.

Marie opened the door like it was her birthday. She opened her arms, gave Ponyboy a huge hug, and said, "We are going to see our allies tonight after dinner." When the night falls, it is very dark out.

Marie looks out the window to see if she can find a shortcut to the Death Rose castle. She did, but they had to walk through water and Marie said, "Well, we have a shortcut. But we have to walk through water, but it is not bad at all."

So, all forty-eight of the towers of fangs got ready to journey to the northwest to meet with the Death Rose clan. However, the two elders said, "We should stay back, in case some of the new-age vampires come from behind and attack us early."

Chapter 7

So, they set off to the path of the shortcut to the northwest to the Death Ruse castle. I hope that the Death Rose elder got their letter

Meanwhile back with Amanda and Becky while they were talking, a black crow sat by the window with a piece of paper. Amanda said to the female under, "There is a black crow at the window with a piece of paper Ho tween his fingers. The elder looked over to the window and walked over to the window to let the black crow in. The black crow tended on the table, left the peace of paper, and flew away. The female walked over to the table, sat down and opened the letter it said to the elders of Death Rose We are going to meet with you at our halfway mark on our five-agreement line if you want us to cross that is fine. However, we need to flak business about these new-age vampires and werewolves too. Sincerely the elder of the Tower of Fangs.

So, the female elder rang the bell to get all her followers into her meeting room, to tell them that we needed to go to our shortcut halfway to meet the Tower of Fangs clan, to decide on what we were going to do. Because it is, one more day before the full red moon comes and we will be Rattling with the new age clans' vamps to meet them Hostway and talk about our plans to defeat these have fort in peace and quiet."

Everyone was gearing up to make sure that the destroyers would not attack them, from behind.

So, the male alder said, "I will stay behind, if they attack from behind, they will have something coming to them."

So about fifty-ame of the Death Rose set off to the shortcut to find it. About four minutes into the walk, they found the shortcut to go to the Tower of Fang's castle.

So, they started on the path, walking on it when it got a lot darker than the nighttime. So they kept a lot closer than they would in the opening, instead of being inhuman for they went right into werewolf form, to not be in their weak form.

So, after about six minutes of walking on the path they saw two signs, one locked like it said Long ways to the city, 3 miles, and Amanda said, "Remember that sign. That is the long way to the Tower of Fang's castle. The other one is the shortcut to their castle." In addition, Amanda did not go into wed form, because she was strong in both forms, she trained herself to the strong on both sides, not just one.

So, the Death Rose were not at their halfway mark yet and they could see the sun come up. But they kept on going. Aawut when the sun, came up, they saw the river that makes the halfway mark and they were out of breath. So, they drank some water and Amanda knelt down on her knees and then drank some tea.

Then Amanda woke up and saw one blue eye and one yellowish eye glow at her and Amanda said, "They are here they are in the cave over there."

So, all the werewolves looked up and saw the cave, even the blue and yellowish eye of a vampire and Ponyboy said, "It is okay to erase over onto our tart."

So, the werewolves and Amanda crossed over into the Tower of Fangs turf. They went inside the cave and all forty-eight vampires were waiting for them to meet with all fifty-one werewolves. So, the queen of the vampires went. over and talked to one of the werewolves and they went over to the other side of the cave to talk to Cherry and Amanda.

Se Amanda said, "I know what this is about. But what are we going to do about this? When the sun goes down tonight, the full red moon will be out and the two stones of the new age will haunt us down."

Cherry said, "Let them because all we have to do is follow this river. It will lead us to end open field about fifteen minutes from here. So please do not worry about anything."

Amanita went to the werewolves that were back into humans to talk to them and said, "There is a field up ahead following this river about fifteen minutes. We will be there. Do you want to help them or not?"

So, the stan came up with an answer and a male person said, "We will help our friends that we share our turf with. They get our respect then. Let them sleep and we will watch out for them and the clan will take turns watching for vampires and werewolves that are not of our kind or friends."

So, all of the vampires went to sleep but Ponyboy did not. He went outside to get fresh air. The sun did not bother him at all. He talked to Amanda to see what plans they were going to make.

Amanda said, "Well we are going to look at the field to see how it is and to see if it is big enough for ninety-nine of us and the other side with about seventy-two. Oh, and they might bring two elders with them too." Ponyboy said, "Well we can go and look at the field to see if it is high enough. But get this. I killed the Questionable elder of the vampires because she was going to attack us early and did not complete her mission at all."

Amanda and Ponyboy walked to the river and started their way to the field about fifteen minutes from where they were now. So, they keep on continuing their walk where it is nighttime in the thick, thick woods. However, where they are camping out it is sunny out, where the woods are less thick for vampires to team around free. Well about ten minutes into the walk, Amanda asked Ponyboy, "You are the master of the Tower of Fangs. Who are you going to be with? Or can I say, who is going to be your lady for the rest of your life?"

Ponyboy said, "I do not know right now."

Amanda looked at Ponyboy and kissed him on the lips. Ponyboy returned the kiss on her lips they continued kissing. Amanda started taking Ponyboy's shirt off, seeing his six-pack, knowing that he was in good shape lying down and having Amanda on the grass looking up at Ponyboy.

Ponyboy takes Amanda's shirt off, kissing her nice soft body, even her neck, knowing she will not bite her. So, he unbuttoned her Panta while she unbuttoned his pants too. Do, they continue kissing and doing other things?

They were stone, smiling at each other, giving one another a kiss on the lips, saying, "I love you."

They continued their walk to the field about five minutes from where they were. They got to the field in Ove minutes and saw some dead animals with bite marks, and claw marks. Amanda said, "Well they are already trying to get under our shin. Trying to take over the turf we have with each other."

Ponyboy said, "I will agree to that. We need to go back and lay a few until tonight when the red full moon comes out. Then it is on with these weakened vampires and werewolves. Let's go back and tell the others."

So, they head back to the cave. While they headed back, Marie and Crystal were talking to each other. Marie said, "I hope that they come back safe and not hurt. However, Amanda is Bood looking for a werewolf. If I get a chance Would kiss her on the lips."

Crystal said, "What do you swing both ways?"

Marin said, "Yes I do. I like girls and guys."

Crystal said, "Okay, just wondering, that's all."

So, one of the werewolves from the Death Rose clan came up to Marie and said, "So how do you like being a vampire and not being like Ponyboy, he is a half-breed for both sides of the field of great strength and power."

Marie said, "I love being a vampire because it fits me and my life. That's why, Anything else sir?"

Then the male werewolf was silent after that little commotion that Marie and him had then.

Amanda and Ponyboy came in and said we needed to be on alert from now on because the questionable and the destroyers were just eating animals and trying to walk on our turf. Then everyone's face was very surprised that they were trying to attack us early and trying to take over our turf when we were sleeping or off guard. So, hours go by, the Tower of Fangs clan is sleeping, and a couple of Death Rose Werewolfs are doing the same next to the door. It was in the evening that Amanda was getting sleepy and nodding off watching for any vampires and werewolves. But she walked war to where Ponyboy was and shook him on thus shoulder to wake him up. Amanda said, "Ponyboy I am sleepy and tired. Can you watch over my shift please?"

Ponyboy was half awake and said, "Okay I will take over your shift to watch over you guys and the vampires and werewolves that we are going to fight tonight."

Amanda went to sleep where Ponyboy was sleeping. It was nice and warm for her to fall asleep.

Chapter 8

About nighttime, before the red full moon comes out Ponyboy is looking around when he sees an elder werewolf that did not look like the elder werewolf that he has a treaty with, he then wakes up everyone. Ponyboy said, "They are here waiting for us, the destroyers, not the Questionable. I did not see any at all when I was looking around."

Amanda looked out of the cave and saw about twenty over to the right of her, waiting for them. Amanda said to everyone, "The destroyers are here, but they are on the right side of us. They wanted to come from behind us. That's how new age werewolves play, not straight up, face to face."

So, it was getting a lot darker out because of the way the woods were getting quiet with the animals. Ponyboy looked up to the sky and saw the red full moon out and all the Death Rose clan people were changing into werewolves. Ponyboy turned into a half-breed vampire/werewolf and others of the tower of Fangs were changing their face to vampire form and showing their fangs.

The Tower of Fangs walked out of the cave; right behind them was the Death Rose clan.

walking on those four legs heading towards the field and the tower of fangs looking at the questionable and the destroyer, when the Death Rese was too. The Tower of Fangs were waiting for this moment to come and to destroy both clans, even the Death Rose was waiting for this moment to help the Tower of Fangs to destroy the other stans that were copying them. The Tower of Fangs and Death Rose were coming up to the open field when they saw about thirty-six vampires of the questionable and thirty-seven werewolves of the destroyers, They were all mixed in, just waiting for the Tower of Fangs and Death Rose.

Ponyboy said, "Let's mix in together Death Rose and defeat these new-age clans for good."

Amanda said, "I will be in front with Ponyboy and everyone is in and help one another. This is going to be a big battle, where it is going to be blood and guts splattered all over everywhere. She stays close to one another."

So, the new-age clans walked towards the old-age clans and they talked and had some words.

Then they walked back and Ponyboy heard one of the werewolves of the destroyer clan say. The half-bread isn't that powerful. He is very wonk.

Se Ponyboy said, "Why don't we start now, and I rip off the one that was talking shit, saying I am weak, I am not come to test my powers on you weak elders of the destroyers."

Ponyboy started to run and Amanda was right behind him and the others. Then Ponyboy leapt in mid-air with the enemy fighting him. Then Ponyboy threw the elder in with everyone crashing and fighting. He flew down looking for the elder. He found him far away, walking near and werewolf.

The elder whispered into the werewolf and said, "Kill Ponyboy! Do not let him live."

Then the werewolf ran very fast and Ponyboy grabbed the werewolf's throat, ripped it out, and yelled "YOU ARE MY ELDER OF THE DESTROYERS DON'T RUN TOO FAR!" Ponyboy ran up a hill and saw the elder running. So, Ponyboy ran and leapt in mid-air and knocked the elder down. Ponyboy landed on these two feet with the taste of blood in his mouth.

THE END